For Ferris and Ursula —TL • *For Jesse —LC*

First US edition 2022. First published by Walker Books Ltd. (UK) 2020. Library of Congress Catalog Card Number 2021946585. ISBN 978-1-5362-1768-1. This book was typeset in Bembo. The illustrations were done in watercolor, acrylic, and pencil. Candlewick Studio, an imprint of Candlewick Press, 99 Dover Street, Somerville, Massachusetts 02144. www.candlewickstudio.com. Printed in Heshan, Guangdong, China. 21 22 23 24 25 26 LEO 10 9 8 7 6 5 4 3 2 1

The Song of the Nightingale

Tanya Landman • ILLUSTRATED BY *Laura Carlin*

CANDLEWICK STUDIO

an imprint of Candlewick Press

The earth was young and fresh and full of color.

By day the golden sun hung in a clear blue sky.
Silvered streams ran down purple mountains
into deep-green seas.

By night the moon lay on a quilt of velvet black,
draped over snowcapped peaks.

There were burning deserts of yellow and orange and flaming red. Shaded forests were filled with trees and flowers in every color of the rainbow.

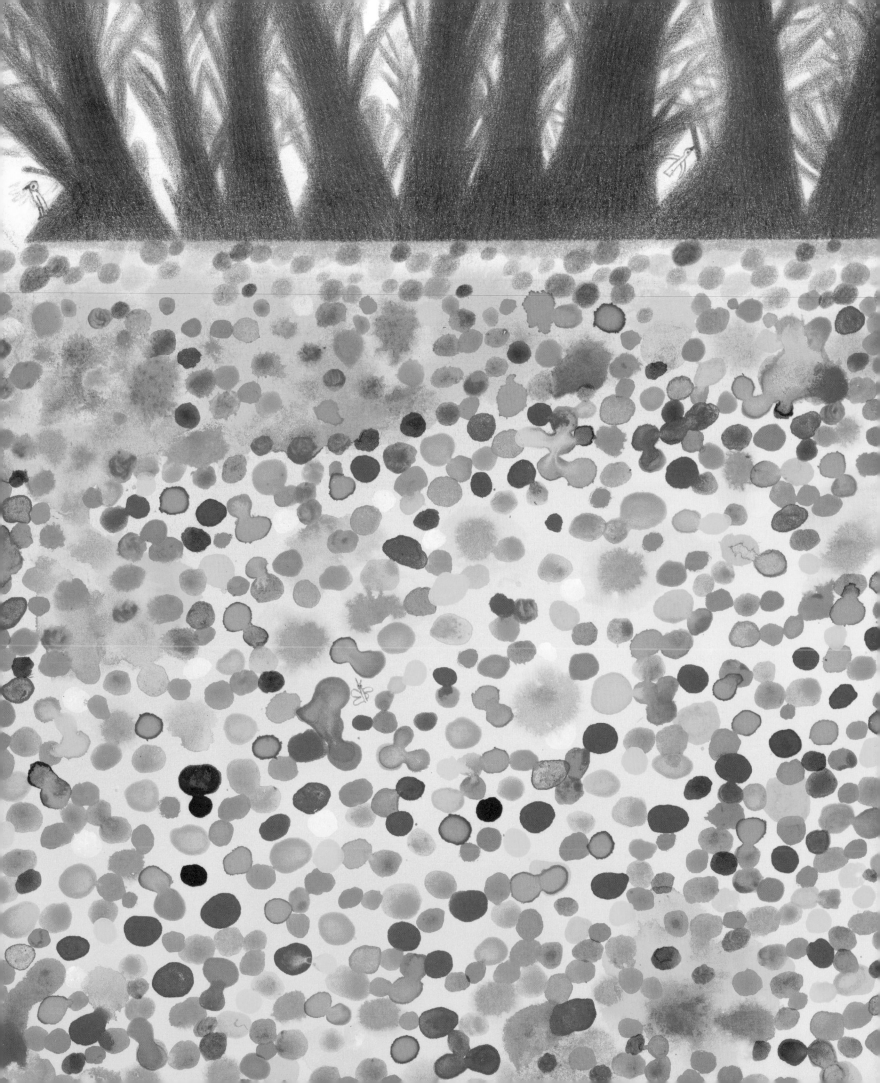

But the animals! They were dull
and drab. So the painter decided:
SOMETHING MUST BE DONE.

She called all the animals
together: snakes with scales
and fish with tails and pigs
with bristly hair. Whales that
swam and deer that ran and birds
that soared through the air.
Leather-winged bats and
sharp-toothed rats and
growly grizzly bears.

The line stretched as far as she
could see. It was going to be
a very long day. The painter
rolled up her sleeves and
opened her paint box.

She started with the itty-bitty animals, dabbing dots on ladybugs and spots on butterflies.

As the morning went on, she slicked stripes
on zebras and painted pentagons on
giraffes. She popped penguins
into sharp suits and furnished
flamingos with feathers
of delicate pink.

The sun was high in the sky
when the painter stopped to rest.
The penguins waddled away and
plopped into the deep, dark seas.
Flamingos took to the air—a rosy
blush across the sky. While the
painter was watching them, a
mandrill sat on her paint box
and ended up with a very
colorful bottom.

The painter went back to work. She'd had enough of persnickety patterns, so she got out her biggest paintbrush and some enormous pots of paint. She painted crocodiles green and elephants gray, kangaroos red and orangutans orange, lions yellow . . .

and whales blue.

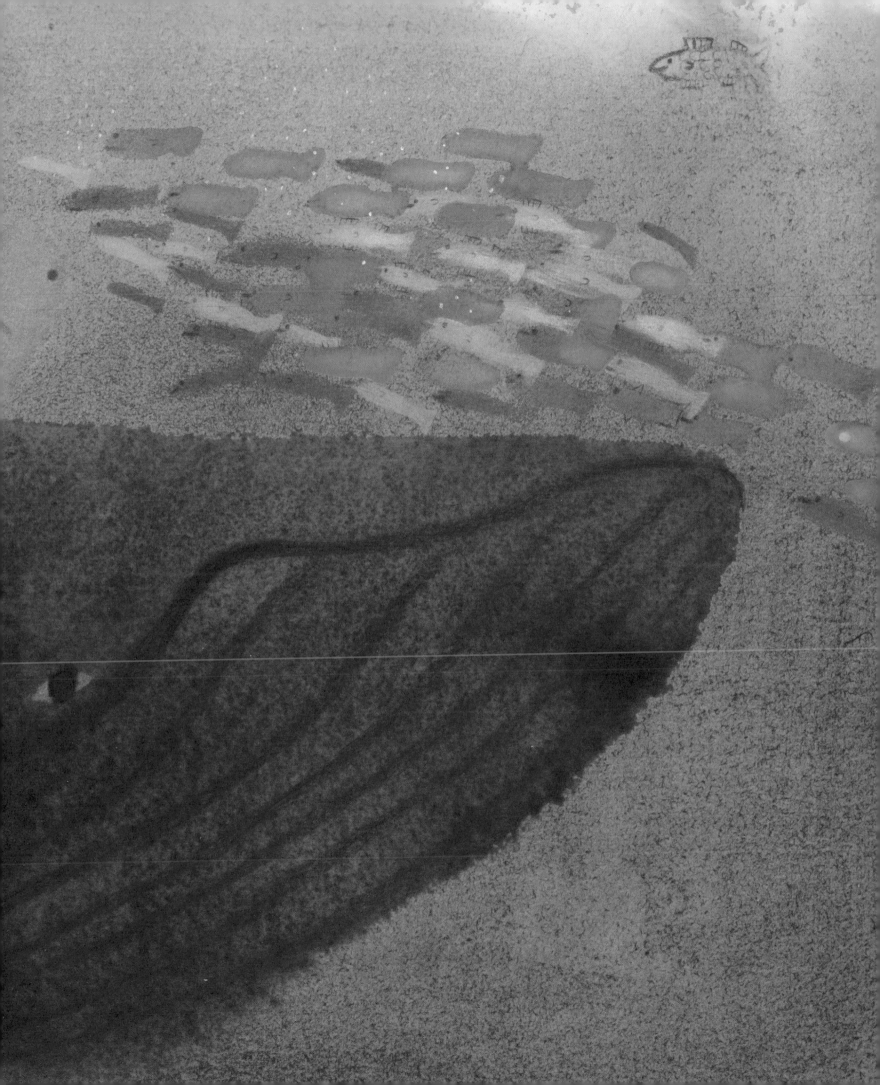

Four birds kept arguing about which of them had been painted the prettiest color. They squawked and shrieked and bumped into one another. Since their paint was still wet, they got splashes of different colors all over themselves.

These were the parrots.

The painter worked all day, animal after animal after animal, until she came to the last one in line. It was a tiny beetle who had waited patiently for its turn. Because it had stood so quietly for so long, the painter took out a tiny pot of gold paint, and that little beetle became the golden scarab.

At last the job was done.

The sun was going down, and it was starting to get dark. The painter closed up her paint box and rolled down her sleeves.

She was just about to go home when out of the shadows of the forest flew a little bird. It had been scared by the noise the animals had made as they lined up to be painted and it didn't like the heat of the bright day. This bird preferred the coolness of evening and the stillness of night. It flew all the way up to the painter and perched on a branch, putting its head on one side and waiting to see what color it would be.

The painter smiled and opened her box. But there was no paint left! She had used all the colors on the other animals. There was nothing left for this little bird.

Then the painter looked at her brush. There on the tip—right on the very end—was a tiny drop of gold paint.

The painter asked the bird to open up its beak, and she put that drop of gold paint right at the back of its throat.

And then the painter
asked the little
bird to sing.

A stream of golden notes tumbled from its throat
and floated into the night. The song was so lovely,
it brought tears of joy to the painter's eyes.

To this day, that little bird prefers the coolness of evening and the stillness of night. When the sun goes down and a velvety darkness covers the earth, it comes out to sing with its beautiful golden voice.

So we call that
little bird the
nightingale.